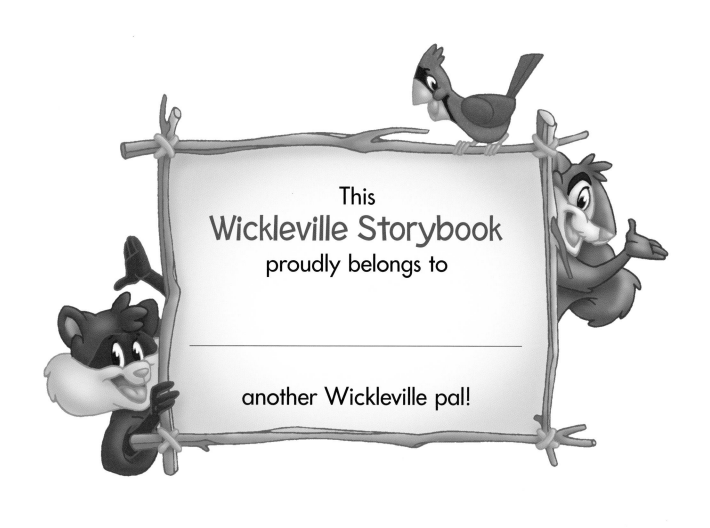

This
Wickleville Storybook
proudly belongs to

_____

another Wickleville pal!

Lynae Wingate, John R. Kober – Editors

Library of Congress Catalog Card Number: 99-69468

ISBN 1-889319-73-2

10 9 8 7 6 5 4 3 2

Squirrels Don't Read, Shakespeare

by Jeffrey Sculthorp

Illustrations by Lorin Walter

WICKLEVILLE WOODS

TREND enterprises, Inc.

Shakespeare the squirrel always wanted to read.

It was so important for him to succeed.

In Wickleville Park, he would watch others read.

Reading looked like more fun than playing in trees.

Thinking this is easy, he picked up a book.

It was 100 ways for nuts to be cooked.

But it made no sense.　　　　　　　He did not understand.

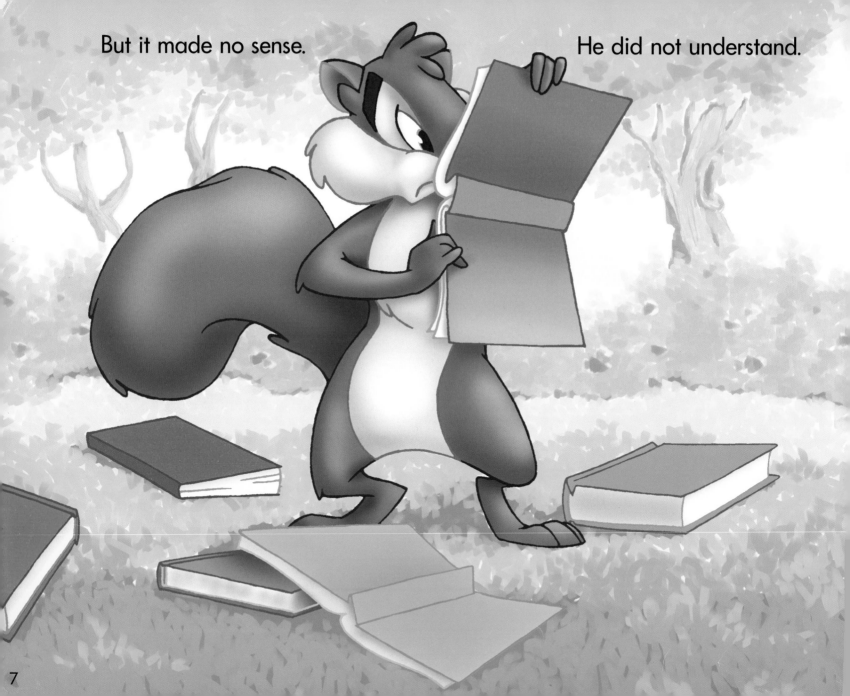

He would have to find help. He needed a hand!

He asked the rabbits, chipmunks, and birds;

but not even the cows could read those strange words.

So he went to find Albert, the smartest owl he knew.

If anyone could help,
Albert would be one of the few.

"Squirrels don't read, Shakespeare.
They eat nuts and look cute.

You should give up and go back to your home. Hoot-hoot!"

"Please help me Albert; I want to read right now!
Then I could teach chipmunks, birds, rabbits, and cows."

"Okay Shakespeare, I will help you read like me,

but first you'll have to learn all your A, B, Cs."

"Even though you're smart, I am sorry to say,

learning how to read will take more than one day."

"You'll have to be patient," he said with a smile.

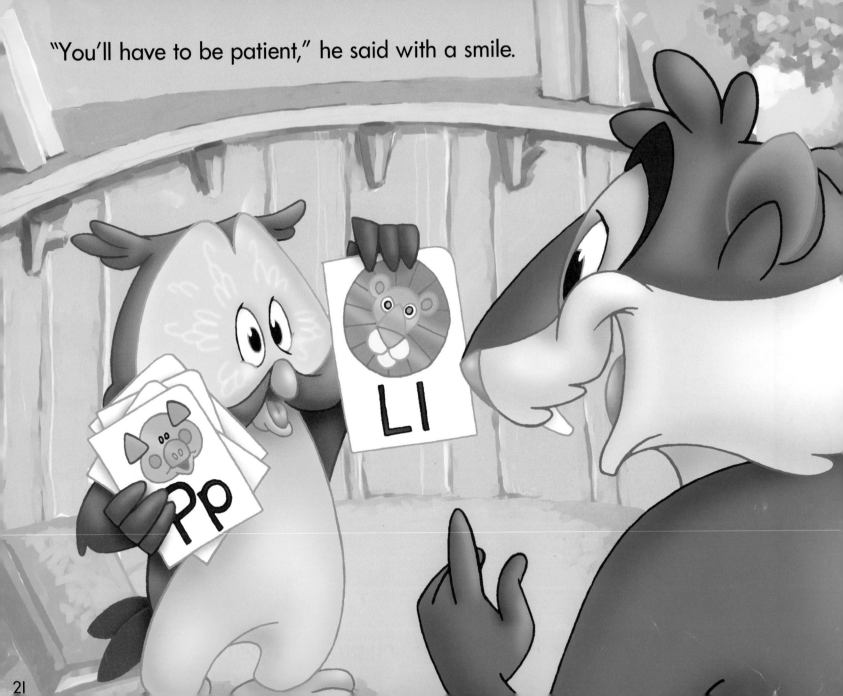

"You'll have to work hard and practice a while."

Shakespeare was excited, and he studied each day.

For the next few months, he had less time to play.

So he worked really hard, and then in the end...